James Hinton

The Mystery of Pain

a book for the sorrowful

James Hinton

The Mystery of Pain
a book for the sorrowful

ISBN/EAN: 9783337780418

Printed in Europe, USA, Canada, Australia, Japan

Cover: Foto ©Andreas Hilbeck / pixelio.de

More available books at **www.hansebooks.com**

THE MYSTERY OF PAIN:

𝔄 𝔅𝔬𝔬𝔨 𝔣𝔬𝔯 𝔱𝔥𝔢 𝔖𝔬𝔯𝔯𝔬𝔴𝔣𝔲𝔩.

"I cried to thee, O Lord, and unto the Lord I made supplication: What PROFIT is there in my blood?"

LONDON:

SMITH, ELDER & CO., 65 CORNHILL.
1866.

To

My Mother,

from whom these thoughts,

not uttered in words, but acted out in life,

have come to me,

I Dedicate

them as her own.

THE MYSTERY OF PAIN.

CHAPTER I.

THIS book is addressed to the sorrowful. It may be there are some in whose lives pleasure so far overbalances pain, that the presence of the latter has never been felt by them as a mystery. It is probable that there are more who, through native strength of mind, or felicity of circumstance, are able to meet the questions that arise out of it with unoppressed hearts, and who have so strong a faith in good that they can, without difficulty, resolve all forms of evil into it. To these I do not address myself; but there is another, and, I think, a more numerous class, to whom their own or others' pain is a daily burden, upon whose hearts it weighs with an intolerable

A

anguish. I seek to speak to these ; not as a teacher, but as a fellow. Sharing their feeling, and knowing well how vain is the attempt to throw off misery, or to persuade ourselves that life is better than it is, I would fain share with them also some thoughts that have seemed to me capable of casting a bright gleam of light athwart the darkness, and, if they are true, of bringing an immense, an incredible joy out of the very bosom of distress.

It seems to me, indeed, that nothing less than this will suffice ; that pain must furnish its own consolation, if it is to be consoled at all ; or rather that it must give more than consolation—that it must give joy. If it can be made fruitful thus, if a rejoicing can be seen to be rooted in sorrow, not sometimes only, but absolutely, then at least one part of the mystery, and perhaps the hardest and the darkest part, would be gone. And this it is that I think I have seen, and that I wish, if I can be so happy, to show to those who need it more than myself, and who better than myself may profit by it.

Let me beg the patience of one class of

sufferers, and their forbearance even, with some of the thoughts which are herein addressed to another. No one, I think, can have had much intercourse with those who have been called upon to suffer, without feeling that there are two different ways in which their pains most heavily assault them. There are some in whom the fact that they and others are called on for endurance—even the endurance of unutterable pains—rouses no angry questionings, and excites no doubts. Their hearts may be bowed down to the earth, but they do not murmur; they think it natural that the ways of God should be beyond mortal fathoming, and that what would seem best to our narrow vision could not be the truly good; in their deepest agony, they do not question righteousness. But there are others—I think they are the more—the chief poignancy of whose sufferings comes from an irrepressible doubt of right, a burning passion to penetrate the impenetrable meaning of their anguish. They might gird themselves up to endure, but they cannot tolerate the unreason, the waste, the seeming wrong. Their souls, which might stand erect before the utterest tortures which right could demand, or reason could inflict, writhe in impotent passion in face of that cold, unanswering law which will spare nothing, or that cruel caprice which lays its sacrilegious choice upon the best. What they demand is to see a right and purpose in the loss and wrong.

It is a human cry, which surely God does not despise. Is it not, indeed, a faith ignorant of itself?—an assurance that there must be in God's world a right, a perfect reason, which would not baulk our hearts or mock our hopes if we could know it? Surely we ought not to be impatient of these demands, even when they are most impatiently urged. Those who do not feel them, or who have succeeded in hushing them within their own bosoms, may permit them to be weighed and pondered to the full for others' sakes. Perhaps, too, it may be found that these passionate questionings do not lead us altogether wrong ; that God's own Spirit may be prompting them, designing to meet them with an answer; that they may be, though a faulty, yet an acceptable, fulfilling of the precept: "For this thing will I be inquired of, saith the Lord." Do not our Saviour's words encourage us to seek knowledge as well as other gifts, when He says, "I call you not servants, but I have called you friends, for all things that I have heard of my Father I have made known unto you."

If we knew all things that the Father does, would our hearts be consoled? would our sorrows be turned into joy? Does not the secret anticipation of the heart, in answer to this question, mark the distinction of the believer and the faithless? I believe that by such knowledge sorrow would be turned into joy; I think it may even be seen that it would; that we may have a knowledge now that proves it. Accustomed as we have been to be in darkness, and to bear sorrow unassuaged (debarred by loss and lapse from our privilege as Christian men,) have we not almost forgotten that the Spirit is the Comforter; that the gospel claims, as one of its chief ends, that we might have great consolation; that God has undertaken Himself to wipe away all tears from His children's eyes; and that Christ, foretelling tribulation, has bidden us be of good cheer?

Let us recall the joyful words; let us assure ourselves that they do verily express the truth; let us be bold to believe them, and, believing them, to look for and to welcome all agencies by which they are fulfilled. From whatever unexpected quarters, or quarters most threatening and hostile, there springs up consolation, may we not believingly recognise it as God's messenger, as His minister for fulfilling His word? Himself not unwilling to do the consoler's part—nay, rejoicing most therein—shall we wonder that He bends all things to the same end, makes all results of human effort, all the long tale of human strife, His ministers, to do for Him His best and dearest work; to give us joy, such joy as His; to transmute our life, and make its dark threads translucent with the splendour of a glory like His own?

Can we wonder if all that man has known or done has been working together, unknown

to him, indeed, but guided by God's hand, to
this end: coming to us now as His ministers in
our sore need, and bringing refreshing waters
to us when we are thirsting unto death? For
surely never was the healing water needed
more than now. Man has learnt many things,
but he has not learnt how to avoid sorrow.
Among his achievements the safeguard against
wretchedness is wanting. Perhaps, indeed, he
could scarcely be charged with exaggeration
who should hold that the aggregate of man's
unhappiness had increased with his increasing
culture, and that the acuter sensibility and
multiplied sources of distress more than out-
weigh the larger area from which his pleasures are drawn, and the more numerous means
of alleviation at his command. At least, it
appears certain that the heaping up of enjoyments, if ever it was designed as a means of
producing happiness, has proved a signal failure. When we regard the general tone of
feeling of our age, whether as expressed in
its literature, in its social intercourse, or even
more, perhaps, in its amusements, do we not
find ourselves in presence of a society from

which real gladness has well-nigh died out, in which hope is almost extinct? I seem to be reminded of the attempt so often made, and proved fruitless just as often, by external pleasures and multiplied distractions to beguile, or at least to quiet, a wounded heart. Man's heart is wounded in these latter days; the bright dreams of his youth have vanished; the outpouring of his deepest passion recoils on himself in mockery; but he can attire himself in gorgeous apparel, and fare sumptuously every day. He can lay all lands under contribution, and make Nature serve his pleasures; he can even explore all knowledge—if he will abstain from asking any question that it truly concerns his manhood to have answered. But surely it is not now an open question whether pampered luxury or gratified curiosity can heal a wounded spirit.

If happiness is to revisit the earth, or, if it have ever been a stranger there, is to be strange no longer, it must come in the form of a genuine joy of heart, a satisfaction of our highest nature. It must come surrounded with light, and bring hope in its train; it must bid our

largest and noblest affections spring up and
blossom anew. It must visit us as spring
visits the frozen lands, and make our life-
blood flow again with a warm current in our
veins.

And there are thoughts which would do
this ; thoughts which are possible to us now :
in some sense, indeed, now first possible to us,
though open to all men since Christ and His
apostles preached. Old thoughts, and yet
new ; as old as the gospel, yet taught us with
fresh evidence. and proof by the last discov-
eries of science, which do but gather up the
testimony of Nature to that good news, and
bid us seek beyond the visible the secret of
our life.

It is true, indeed, that no change in our
thoughts can alter the nature of things, or
invert the essential relations of pleasure and
pain. No form of opinion can make bitter
sweet, or cause the couch of suffering to be a
grateful rest. Yet let us observe what is true,
on the other hand. It is in the power of
knowledge very radically to determine our
feelings, and sometimes to make the same

things in a high degree pleasurable, or the reverse. Take, for example, the case of hypocritical pretence of friendship, and designing arts to procure our favour. Ignorant of their nature, these pretensions (if not too gross) might be sources of gratification to us ; but the discovery of their true character makes them in the highest degree repulsive, nothing being altered but our knowledge. A similar effect may be produced in the opposite direction : the apparent aversion or coldness of a beloved person may be turned into a source of joy, if it be discovered to depend upon a real regard.

It is in the power, therefore, of the discovery of an unknown or unregarded fact to alter our feelings—even to invert their natural character ; to make unpleasing that which is naturally pleasant, or to render in the highest measure joyful that which is naturally·repugnant. This power is in knowledge where there has been ignorance. It does not alter our natural emotions : it still leaves (as in the cases supposed) the manifestations of regard agreeable in themselves, and the tokens of aversion in themselves the source of pain; but it can overrule these primary tendencies, eliciting feelings which are stronger within us than the sensational impressions. We may take another simple case: The loss of a small sum of money is a naturally painful thing; few persons could avoid a distinct emotion of annoyance from its occurrence. But let a generous man discover that through that loss a dear friend has been largely benefited, and his feeling is entirely changed; the vexation is lost in a stronger pleasure.

It is therefore evident that knowledge might alter our whole feeling with respect to. the world. The apparent good and evil of life constitute a case in which a truer understanding might invert the natural impression. We need not, therefore, be hopeless in presence of the problem of pain. Knowledge might alter its entire aspect. Nay, we are not limited to this general thought. For there is one condition under which all know that pain is not truly an evil, but a good. This is when pain is willingly borne for another's sake. Its entire character is altered then. It not only passes into the category of good things, but it becomes emphatically *the good*. Our life has nothing else so excellent to show. All kinds of pleasure fall infinitely below it. Measured by self-sacrifice, by heroism, every other good sinks not only into a lower place, but becomes evidently of a lower kind. Nothing else in the same full and perfect sense deserves or receives the name of good. The homage of all hearts unequivocally affirms this title. Even when there is not manhood enough to imitate, when the baser nature within us prefers the meaner course, the verdict of the soul is never doubtful. The pains of martyrs, or the losses of self-sacrificing devotion, are never classed among the evil things of the world. They are its bright places rather, the culminating points at which humanity has displayed its true glory, and reached its perfect level. An irrepressible pride and gladness are the feelings they elicit: a pride which no regret can drown, a gladness no indignation overpower. Conceive all martyrdoms blotted out from the world's history; how blank and barren were the page!

There are the materials, then, evidently within us for an entire inversion of our attitude towards pain. The world in this respect, we might almost feel, seems to tremble on the balance. A touch might transform it wholly. One flash of light from the Unseen, one word spoken by God, might suffice to make the dark places bright, and wrap the sorrow-stricken heart of man in the wonder of an unutterable glory.

If all pain might be seen in the light of martyrdom; if the least and lowest in man's poor and puny life—or shall we rather say, in God's great universe—might be interpreted by its best and highest, were not the work done? It is done: for the light has shone, the word is spoken.

CHAPTER II.

A BRIEF narrative of my thoughts may
be allowed me, as the simplest method
I can adopt of giving them expression. Some
time ago, two feelings were forcibly impressed
upon my mind. On the one hand, I was made
conscious afresh of the evil that is in man's
present state; an evil deeply affecting his
whole being, and demanding for its remedy
·nothing less than a reconstruction and restoration of his nature. And, on the other hand, I
was scarcely less impressed with the evidence
that there exists in all human experience
something unseen, some fact beyond our consciousness, so that the seeming of our life is
not the truth of it.

Neither of these thoughts is new. They
came with new force to my mind owing to
particular lines of thought on which I was
engaged, which presented them to me in fresh
lights, and with new evidence, making old
words burn with a new lustre; but they are

in themselves familiar truths. The radical need of a change in human nature has been affirmed by the best members of the human race, as long as history records the thoughts of men : with us it has become mixed up with theologic doctrines, and so has been made the subject of verbal disputes ; but it is itself an old and native feeling of the human heart.

And the belief that there is an unseen fact beneath all that we are conscious of—that there is something unperceived by us which gives rise to all our experience—also is not new ; though it has lately taken a more distinct form and place in the human mind.

They are two old and customary thoughts ; but the freshness with which they appeared to me enabled me to see in them a relation which I had not perceived before. That which suggested itself to me was this : If man's nature needs a change, and there is some fact we are not conscious of causing our experience, then may not this fact be the working of that very change in man ?

This thought assumed by degrees in my mind the character of an assured and manifest truth.   It is the starting point from which the thoughts contained in this volume sprang :—

Our experience is the working out of a change in man ; or, to speak in clearer and more familiar terms, it is the carrying out of man's redemption.

It is clear that if this thought could be accepted as the truth, it would fulfil the conditions for a complete change in our thought of life.   To connect all our experience with such an end would enable us to read it entirely anew.   For by giving to our pains a place of use and of necessity, not centred on ourselves, but extending to others, and indeed affecting others chiefly, as existing for, and essential to, God's great work in the world ;—by giving to our painful experience this place, its whole aspect would be altered.   It would come within the sphere of that pain which is capable of being the instrument of joy ; which exhibits the highest good we can in our present state attain,—the pain, that is, of martyrdom and sacrifice.   Nor are we left indeed to rest merely in this general thought : it comes to us realised in the highest form, and raises our souls to a height which might seem too awful and too full of joy. For so regarded, all our pains—all human pain and loss—identify themselves, in meaning and in end, with the sufferings of Christ. He stands as the Revealer to us of Human Life; and the emotions which His story awakens within us become the pattern of those with which all distress may be encountered and every loss accepted.

And surely we may at least say this: If God would give us the best and greatest gift, that which above all others we might long for and aspire after, even though in despair, it is this that He must give us, the privilege He gave His Son, to be used and sacrificed for the best and greatest end. Nothing else could so fill our nature or satisfy our hearts as this; that Christ's own life should be renewed, His work fulfilled in us; that we should be united with Him *so*, and feel the wonderful words of St Paul true of our own poor and blank-seeming sorrows: " I fill up that which is behind of the afflictions of Christ, for His body's sake, which is the Church:" our suffer-

ings being related to an end that is not merely
ours ; an end that is of all ends the greatest
and the best.

For we are so made as to rejoice in others'
good, to find in it, indeed, our highest joy,
to rejoice, above all, in serving it.   And if this
thought of human life is true, we see that
the gospel addresses man as constituted thus.
Surely it should do so.   If it came to us on
any other ground, it would be addressing itself not only to lower but to weaker elements
within us.   It would pass by the worthiest
part of us, the part most kindred to itself.
For with what light does the gospel come,
what revelation does it make, but this, that
GOD'S highest joy is in others' good ? nay,
that His great heart is impatient of their
misery, and springs forward with an eager
haste to take it on Himself, finding therein
alone the means to make us know Him.

When we look there, we can see why God
is the blest, the happy Being.   We should be
happy if we had love, and found for it such a
work ; if we might take the human sorrow,
and bear it on our hearts, and give our lives,

too, and our sorrows for the redemption of
the world. If we might undertake that work,
a small, the smallest, part of it, and live for
that and die for it, that would be God's greatest gift to us.

His best gift, then, would be, not in our
pleasures but in our sorrows; in our losses
and evils, not in our possessions or delights.
If this one fact of the use of our lives by God
in the redemption of the world were true, the
very foundations of our life would be changed,
the current of our thought and feeling must
pour itself through a new channel.

The view, then, that I desire to suggest
rests upon these two thoughts: that there is
something accomplished in our experience
which is unseen by us; and that sacrifice for
others is a good. For this unseen work that
is done through us is something done for
others.

With this view I think we shall find hereafter that both the facts of life and the constitution of our own nature so evidently agree
as to give it the greatest possible confirmation.
But I may first say a few words respecting

the demand which is thus made upon us to recognise the existence of an unseen fact in all that we experience.

It is evident that all the effects of the events with which we are concerned are not, and could not possibly be, perceived by us. We see and feel things—alike the great ones and the small ones, as we esteem them—only as they affect our senses; that is, only in small part and for a short time. They soon pass beyond our sight, and while they are within it they never show us all they are, often those which are the greatest seeming to us the least. How little we are able, often, to calculate the influence even upon our own future of events or actions of which we seem to have the most perfect knowledge at the time. And of the effects of these events on others, which must go on, so far as we can estimate, without any end, only the smallest fragment is within our view. It is one of the first lessons taught men by experience, not to judge of events by what they seem, alone, but to remember that there may be much more involved in them than appears. To judge of our life, therefore, merely by that which is seen of it, is to commit ourselves to certain error.

So that the thought I have suggested, that in all our experience there is some unseen relation to spiritual things—to a spiritual work in man—makes on us no new demand. It is but the carrying out to their legitimate, and surely to their natural result, principles which experience has established. We shall be sure to be thinking and feeling falsely respecting our life, if we cannot recognise some unseen bearing of it. For we do not, we know we cannot, see the whole.

And this principle is established not only by experience; it is the lesson which, almost more than any other, science teaches us also. In exploring the material world, we soon find that, in order to understand any part of it aright, we must recognise things which are unseen, and have regard to conditions or to actions which do not come within our direct perception. It is enough to instance the pressure of the air, of which we have no consciousness, the motion of the earth, equally

unperceivable by us; the hidden force, lurk-
ing in unseen·atoms, of chemical affinity, or
electricity; the vibrations which traverse the
universal ether; and, in fine, that invisible
unity which makes all her forces one, whereby (holding to the unseen) man has traced
out in nature a perfect order amid all con-
fusion.

So far we have learnt, that what we directly
and naturally perceive in the things around
us, and the events which happen to us, was
never meant to be the guide to our thoughts
respecting them. A chief part of the value
of science, indeed, consists in bringing into
our knowledge, and so into our practical use,
that which is not within our consciousness,
and which our senses can only indirectly, or
even not at all, perceive. Scientific knowledge consists in regarding the unseen; in
looking at things which are in one sense invisible. It is therefore true, because it fulfils
this evident condition for the attainment of
the truth.

And thus, when it is said that all human
experience is the working out of the redemp-

tion of the world, the restoration and perfecting of man's being, it is no difficulty in the way, or evidence to the contrary, that it is not visibly so. If this seem like a difficulty, it arises only from our natural tendency to limit our thoughts by our impressions, and so to condemn ourselves to error. That is the one source of error from which all advance in knowledge sets us free; it is the one difficulty which obstructs the road to truth. Reference is made to an unseen fact. It should be so. If the fact were not unseen, it could not be the truth; for it would not be freed from the limitations of our perception. This does but bring the thought into harmony with all our thoughts that we have just ground for believing true. And if a certain effort is demanded to free ourselves from the dominion of our own too small impressions, it is but the same effort which is, or has been, the condition of all knowledge. But here the effort is not intellectual. We are not called upon by great stretch of thought to see relations in ordinary facts which no common eye can see. We are not bidden to follow causes to far

distant and remote effects. The demand is
not for a larger intellectual view, but for
faith ; for that which is the common and
inevitable basis of all religion, and is the
foundation-stone of Christianity. We have
to recognise a fact no human eye, indeed, can
fully trace, but which God reveals.

CHAPTER III.

A CONSIDERATION of the uses that pain visibly serves in human life may add weight to the thoughts that have been suggested. For these uses, which have been often dwelt upon, are by far too limited, even if they were otherwise adapted, to give the key to its existence. Three uses of pain are recognised, and indeed cannot be overlooked :—

1. Bodily pain prompts us to many actions which are necessary for the maintenance or security of life, and warns us against things that are hurtful. It has been often pointed out how largely that which contributes to health is attended with pleasure, and how constantly the access or the causes of disease are accompanied by pain. Cold and hunger, for example, lead us to feed and clothe ourselves, and when excess begins, there come satiety and disgust.

These things are true, but they exhibit only

one side of the facts. If pain is in these re-
spects often beneficial, it is also often harmful;
and in almost all cases it is liable to exceed,
in an immense degree, the amount which is
needful to secure its beneficial influence. The
pain of many diseases, by the exhaustion it
produces, is one of the chief sources of their
danger; while in many cases, as in the abuse
of intoxicating drinks, it wholly fails to indicate the most fatal perils.

And not only is life, in many cases, crowded
with useless or excessive pains, but our sensibility itself seems to be more developed for
pain than for pleasure. Is not our power of
suffering in excess of our power of enjoying?
Intense enjoyment can last but for a short
time, and when once the limit of fatigue is
reached, the pleasure itself may become a
source of torture; but pain may continue
undiminished, even growing in severity, until
life itself succumbs.

Indeed, if we bring ourselves resolutely to
look at all the facts, are we not almost compelled to feel that our nature—at least our
bodily nature—is constituted rather for pain

than for pleasure ? It is to the former that it vibrates, if not most readily, at least most intensely and most protractedly. Nor can we overlook here that strange law of our constitution by which a comparatively slight pain will spoil much happiness, and even turn what should be pleasure into bitterness.

There is no adequate explanation, therefore, to be found of pain in the beneficial effects which it produces in respect to our physical existence. It serves these uses—is benevolently meant to serve them, doubtless, as our hearts irrepressibly affirm—but it exists independently of them. Its source lies deeper, and its ends are larger.

2. But, secondly, pain serves as a punishment for sin ; it follows wrongdoing, in the forms of bodily disease or want, of mental anguish, or social vengeance. Suffering is the minister of justice. This is true in part, yet it also is inadequate to explain the facts. Of all the sorrow which befalls humanity, how small a part falls upon the specially guilty ; how much seems rather to seek out the good ! Nights spent in dissipation bring ruined health ;

nights spent in fond watchings by beds of pain bring a like and equal ruin. To what sufferings children are subject, and indeed all who are not able to protect themselves! We might almost ask whether it is not weakness rather than wrong that is punished in this world?

Nor is there a wider basis for the idea that physical pain punishes the violation, not of moral, but of physical law. Not to speak of the cruelty which thus inflicts the last punishment upon the ignorant, and treats misfortune as a crime, the relation is itself as partial as the others. No violated physical law can be shown in destruction by storm or earthquake, or in the poverty which presses upon the weaker members of a thickly peopled country. Pain avenges the majesty of violated law, physical and moral, but it does not exist for this.

3. But there is another end which pain fulfils, a worthier and more satisfying one, perhaps, than either of those that have been mentioned. It disciplines and corrects the erring, chastens and subdues the proud, weans from false pleasures, teaches true wisdom.

Happily it does; but only in some cases. Unhappily it more often fails to teach or to subdue. Often it hardens or perverts. Pain is used for a discipline, but can we say that it exists solely for that end when those to whom it is no blessing, but a curse, whom it rouses only to bitterness, or sinks merely into despair, have no exemption, and seem to plead in vain for pity? Most often in this sad world pain works, to our eyes, evil, and not good; and where it works no good, it often falls most heavily. Some other source and reason must be found for pain than the moral benefit it visibly brings the sufferer.

And if neither of the uses we have thus observed in pain can even seem to furnish the reason for its existence, so neither can they when taken altogether. There are pains innumerable which benefit neither the body nor the soul; which punish no moral wrong, which vindicate no material law against voluntary breach. Take, for one instance, the sufferings of industry condemned to reluctant idleness, which lead so often to discontent and bitterness of heart.

All these we have enumerated are secondary purposes served by pain. They do not conduct us to its source, nor reveal to us its meaning. Neither does the fact that the progress of man and the development of his powers are prompted and maintained by the discomforts and evils which he feels. For pain often paralyses instead of stimulating, and reduces to impotence energies of the utmost value.

We must, therefore, accept pain as a fact existing by a deep necessity, having its root in the essential order of the world. If we are to understand it, we must learn to look on it with different eyes. And does not a different thought suggest itself even while we recognise that the others fail? For if the reason and the end of pain lie beyond the results that have been mentioned, then they lie beyond the individual. Pain, if it exist for any purpose, and have any end or use—and of this what sufferer can endure to doubt?—must have some purpose which extends beyond the interests of the person who is called upon to bear it. For the ends which have been mentioned include all that concerns the individual himself. That which surpasses these rises into a larger than the individual sphere. From this ground it becomes evident again that, to know the secret of our pains, we must look beyond ourselves.

These uses of pain, which concern the one who suffers only, must fail and be found insufficient; they ought not to be enough, for they do not embrace that which is unseen. Confining ourselves to that which is visible to us, we ought to find ourselves in darkness, unable to answer irrepressible questions. But when we extend our thought, and recognise not only that there are, in pain, ends unseen by us, but that these ends may not be confined within the circle of our own interests, surely a light begins to glimmer through the darkness. While we look only at that which directly concerns the individual who suffers, no real explanation of suffering, no satisfaction that truly satisfies, can be found. But if we may look beyond, and see in our own sufferings, and in the sufferings of all, something in which mankind also has a stake, then they are brought into a region in which the heart can deal with them and find them good. And if the heart, the reason also. For here it is the soul that is the judge ; and if the heart is satisfied, the reason also is content.

CHAPTER IV.

WE have noticed before how love is capable in some degree of overruling our natural feelings of pain, and of making some things, that otherwise would be painful, a source of joy to ourselves, if they are productive of benefit to others whom we delight to serve. When we look into this subject farther, we see that it is a law of our experience that our own mental condition controls and even alters our feelings. Though we speak of pleasure and pain as fixed and definite things, yet they are truly by no means fixed. It is matter of familiar experience that various circumstances may modify our sensibility in respect to things which are, in our ordinary state, painful. The power of mental excitement in this respect is well known. A soldier wounded during battle may feel no immediate suffering from the severest injury; and we have everyday proof of the same thing in the failure of slight accidents to pain us when we are intently occupied. All strong emotions, indeed, seem to have a similar power. It can scarcely be doubted that martyrs have sometimes gone through their flaming death in ecstasy. And the accounts we have of that fanatical sect in the East, one part of whose devotions consists in working themselves first into a frenzy, and then laying hold on glowing iron, dancing with it in their hands, and putting it to their lips, indicate not only an absence of pain in the act, but even some kind of pleasure.

It would seem, indeed, that there is nothing that can be said to be always or necessarily a cause of pain. What we can truly say on this point is, that there are certain things which are painful to our bodily senses when these are not controlled or modified by the state of the mind. It is as truly our nature *not* to feel pain from the ordinarily painful things at some times, as it is to feel them painful at others. In this respect, the power of love to take away pain is not peculiar. Love, when it is strong, can banish pain; but in this it is only like all strong emotions: it is peculiar in its power of making what is ordinarily painful a source of joy, and this a joy of the highest and most exquisite kind. We all know this. We not only are willing, we rejoice, to bear an ordinarily painful thing for the benefit or pleasure of one whom we intensely love. Within certain limits, indeed, but still most truly, the bearing pain for such an end is a privilege to be sought, not a sorrow to be shunned. Universal experience proves this : it is one of the broad familiar features of human life.

But when we consider this, do we not see that our natural feelings mislead us when they pronounce pleasant things to be the good ones, and the painful ones evil? So far from this being the case, things that we call painful, that are painful in our ordinary state, are essential conditions of our highest good. To us, there could not be love without them. We could never have felt the joy, never have had even the idea, of love, if sacrifice had been impossible to us. In our truest and intensest happiness, that which is otherwise felt as pain is present. Pain, we may say, is *latent*, in our highest state. It lies hidden and unfelt in the form of devoted sacrifice; but it is there, and it would make itself felt as pain if the love which finds joy in bearing it were absent. Take, for example, the offices rendered with joy by a mother to her babe: let the love be wanting, and what remains? Not mere indifference, but vexation, labour, annoyance. A gladly-accepted pain is in the mother's love; it is in all love that does not contradict the name. To take away from us the possibility of that which we feel as pain were to take its best part from life, to render it almost—surely altogether—worthless. The possibility of love is given to us in our power of sacrifice; and loving brings the power into immediate action.

To beings constituted as we are the possibility of love can be given only through the power of sacrifice. Our highest happiness consists in the feeling that another's good is purchased by us, that we—our labour or our loss—are the instrument through which it is conferred. Take away that element, and the joy alters its character, and becomes inevitably less. We may still rejoice and be glad in the good fortune of the beloved object, but we can no more rejoice in giving it at our own expense.

In our best happiness, then, what we otherwise term pain is swallowed up. It is embodied and mixed up in the joy. For do we not despise and loathe a man whose only thought in that which he calls love is of the pleasure he can receive? And further, by taking away the love, its sacrifices would be felt as pain: pain emerges, or comes out, from this joy by a taking away, or absence. And its presence, to one who *should* be loving, might imply no evil state around him, but only something wanting in himself. For the very same things may be to us either painful, or in the highest degree productive of delight, of a delight which could not be without them.

Remembering these things, then, what should we consider the presence of pain in the world to mean? Does it not mean that there is a want in man by which that becomes painful which should be joy? Does it not mean that a world in which so much of pain is present, is adapted—was altogether made—to be the scene of an overpowering, an absorbing love?

One element of the best happiness is given, namely, sacrifice : what does it imply but that the other should be present too ?—the other, which is love.

Let us think, then, of ourselves : our natural feeling prompts us to exclude all painful things ; to found a bliss upon their absence. But is not this an utter error, and were not its achievement fatal ? Surely a truer knowledge lays its fullest and intensest grasp upon the painful elements of life, and holds them as the fundamental conditions of its joy. The reason we are made, or seem as if we were made, for pain, is that we are made for love ; the predominance of sacrifice is a sign and proof upon how good a plan the world was formed ; upon how high a type of bliss. Our feeling it as pain, proves something wanting in ourselves.

Doubtless we are right to loathe and repudiate pain, and count its endurance an evil. To be happy is good : to feel pain is evil, and the sign of evil. God meant us for the one, meant us to abhor, and shrink from the other. But the question is, What is the happiness

God has meant us for, the happiness to which human nature is fitted, to which it should aspire? Should it be that from which the painful is banished, or that in which pain is latent? Should pain be merely absent, or swallowed up in love and turned to joy?

Surely we can answer but in one way. To wish the former were to choose the lesser good, to cut ourselves off from our chief prerogative. If God truly loved man, must He not have made him such, that by want of love pain should arise; and that to him—ignorant and unloving as he is—the world should be one dark mystery of sorrow? How else should He have made us capable of joy, how else have made earth tolerable in the eyes of heaven?—in the eyes of that heaven which gazes on the Lamb that has been slain, and sees, unamazed, in Him the brightness of the Father's glory, the express image of His person.

For if in the only worthy joy (the only happiness which, matching the dignity of man or filling his capacity, rightly deserves the name of human,) if in this there is necessarily latent the element of pain, so that by an absence it

must be felt;—if in human joy pain is ab-
sorbed and taken up, not merely excluded or
set aside, then we at once rise in our thoughts
above ourselves.   If this is our joy, then it is
His also in whose image we were made.   The
pain that is latent in man's bliss is latent, too,
in God's; in His most as He is highest: and
that great life and death to which the eyes of
men are ever turned, or wandering ever are
recalled, reveals it to us.

We see it must be so.   If God would show
us Himself, He must show us Himself as a
sufferer, as taking what we call pain and loss.
These are His portion; from eternity He chose
them.   The life Christ shows us is the eternal
life.   He emptied Himself, and the pain became manifest; He put off His perfection, and
the sorrow was hidden and lost in the fulness
of His life no more.   It was revealed as sorrow, becoming visible to human eyes; pierc-
ing the immortal heart before a breathless
world, which, seeing Him, sees and knows the
Father.

Thus our own experience may solve for us
the problem, how God is incapable of suffer-

ing, and yet reveals Himself to us as a sufferer. The seeming contradiction here is only that which the intellect encounters in everything that is true of our own life. Love cannot be explained, made manifest of what nature it is, the secret of its happiness revealed, except by an exhibition of the toil, the abnegation, the sacrifice, that are in it. Seeking for happiness, craving for good, we grasp at pleasure and turn away from pain. God must teach us better, and to do so He shows us the root and basis of His own. Stripping off His infinitude, and taking infirmity like ours, He bids us look and see! The only happiness He has, or can bestow, bears martyrdom within it. If He does not suffer, it is only that His life is perfect ; His love has no hindrance, no shortcoming, and can turn *all* sacrifice to joy. He stands our great example, not exempting Himself from toils and sacrifices which He lays on us, binding heavy burdens, and grievous to be borne, upon men's shoulders, Himself not touching one ; but with so large a heart accepting them, that they are transfigured into the very brightness of His glory,

and our dim eyes cannot discern them, save
as they are shown us with the brightness
veiled, the glory banished, the love itself
subdued to a less burning flame. Revealed
therein in strong crying and tears, that recall
our own experience to ourselves, He makes
us know with which part of it to link His
name. It is sacrifice binds us to God, and
makes us most like Him : sacrifice that to us
is sorrow, wanting life and love ; but to Him,
supreme in both, is joy.

And when we say pain is an evil, we can
only rightly mean that *our feeling it to be pain*
is an evil. That marks defect and want, failure of our proper manhood, shortcoming from
our privilege of joy. From pain we may well
seek and pray to be delivered ; but by what
deliverance ? It may be banished in two
ways—by taking away, or by adding. Pain
may be removed passively by the removal of
that which is its cause, letting us relapse into
mere repose, which may seem joy by contrast,
or by the deadening of the sensibility, that
shall banish alike pain and pleasure. But it
may also be removed actively, positively ; not

by the absence of the cause nor by diminished feeling, but by a new and added power, which shall turn it into joy—a joy like God's.

In the presence of pain the basis is laid of an exquisite delight; should we not seek it? Should we not believe that God will give it? If the thought seems too great for us, is it not therefore more befitting Him, more like what we have learnt of Him? And if He must new-create us in order to give us happiness like this, has He not promised to create us anew? Nay, do we not find here confirmation of His promise, finding our need for its fulfilment?

Since love, then, is in sacrifice, we see that to creatures such as we are, failing of our manhood, pain must be. We see that our Maker, assuming our condition in order that we may know Him, also assumes, and must assume, our sorrow, pre-eminent therein. We see, too, that deliverance from pain must be wrought out within: it must be by a change of life, and not of circumstance. However the latter may be altered, till love itself shall change this fact can never alter—that only in the form of that which we call sacrifice can our true good be given us. Whatever else may pass or change, of this we may be sure, that till God cease to love us we shall stand face to face with sacrifice. Of this, as of our Maker's presence, we may say, "If I ascend into heaven, thou art there : if I make my bed in Hades, behold, thou art there. If I take the wings of the morning, and dwell in the uttermost parts of the sea, even there shall thy hand lead me, and thy right hand shall hold me ;" for where God is, there is love.

CHAPTER V.

THESE thoughts have been made clearer to my own mind by some others which our common experience has suggested to me. My attention was first drawn to them in this connexion while engaged in gardening, and feeling how essential a part of the pleasure which that occupation gave was furnished by the slight inconveniences which it involved. Without the latter, I felt that the employment would have wanted very much of its zest. The little claim upon the endurance constituted a real part of the charm. As I became conscious of this fact, it was natural to go on to reflect how completely it seems to be a law of our nature, that, in order to be thoroughly enjoyable, and to continue so, our life must include more or less of willingly-accepted inconvenience. This inconvenience may be, in most cases, slight, but still (with some exceptions which I shall refer to presently) it seems to be in all cases necessary. There is inconvenience overcome, endurance accepted, to some extent, in every life that is permanently pleasurable ; and this, independently of all moral considerations, merely by the nature of our constitution. We see this fact strikingly exhibited in field sports, and in every kind of active amusement. It reaches its height, perhaps, in the pleasure found now so widely in ascending mountains, which seems to be a really painful task ; but the same element is found almost universally in sports. Look at the roughness and fatigue of cricket, the toil, and even pain, of a hard day's boating. Nay, how much less charm were there even in a pic-nic, if it were not for its inconveniences and little denials.

But these are only special instances of a law that seems to be universal in our experience. Whether it may seem paradoxical or not, it is a fact in our nature that, without endurance, life ceases to be enjoyable ; without pains accepted, pleasure will not be permanent. For the most part, among intelligent persons, this fact is so fully accepted and

acted upon, that they are hardly conscious
how universally it is true. They take their
inconveniences, accept their little pains—let
us say, for example, the rising at a reasonable
hour in spite of sloth, or the free use of cold
water in spite of the shock—and reap their
reward accordingly in a healthful, pleasurable
life. But the law becomes evident immedi-
ately in its breach ; it asserts itself inevitably
against the attempt to avoid it. A life from
which everything that has in it the element of
pain is banished, becomes a life not worth
having ; or worse, of intolerable tedium and
disgust. There is ample proof in the experience of the foolish among the rich, that no
course is more fatal to pleasure than to suc-
ceed in putting aside everything that can call
for endurance. The stronger and more generous faculties of our nature, debarred from
their true exercise, avenge themselves by
poisoning and embittering all that remains.
A striking illustration of this fact is given in
the words reported to have been uttered by
Lord Queensbury as he stood looking at the
scene from Richmond Hill :—" Oh, that wea-

risome river! it will keep running, running, and I so tired of it."*

But the records of luxury in all ages furnish a long succession of similar instances. And the whole principle is embodied in the now universally recognised doctrine of the necessity of work—itself an irksome thing—for happiness.

This is the thought that occurred to me: In our healthful and natural life *endurance* is essential to pleasure. Our enjoyment, by the very construction of our nature, absorbs, and takes into itself as a necessary element, a certain amount of pain; that is, of what would, if it stood by itself, be pain. But when we recognise this fact, we can hardly help remarking another also. The amount of endurance or pain that our pleasure will thus absorb, and turn into its own sustenance, is not fixed. It varies, being in some cases more, and in some less; and especially it varies with the intensity and perfectness of the life. A strong and healthy person can absorb into his pleasure a really large

* Mrs Trench's Memoirs.

amount of what would otherwise be pain, that of a hard day's hunting or rowing, or the ascent of a considerable mountain ; or he will enjoy a great amount of *risk*, as we read in the life of Stephenson, that the navvies in his day preferred the most dangerous tasks. A weak person can enjoy much less—fatigue or discomfort soon spoils his pleasure ; but a sick person, one in whom the bodily life is depraved or wanting in its perfectness, can enjoy none. His pleasure can absorb no endurance at all. He must be shielded from all that is painful, from all that taxes, and to the strong man so delightfully taxes, the power to bear. The pains which are the very conditions of enjoyment to the healthy man, become to him intolerable, utterly unendurable and terrible. He must be laid upon a soft bed, guarded from every shake or jar, from every call upon his powers, from all loud sounds, or brightness even of the light. He can find pleasure only in that which is itself unendurable to the healthy man, the absence of all exertion.

For when we go on to consider the facts in

this connexion, we see that the sick ·man finds intolerable, not only that element in healthy pleasure which demands endurance, and might be regarded as in itself painful, but that every kind of action (speaking generally) is painful to him. The natural exercise of the powers, which is the very source of healthy pleasure, is his agony. His whole feeling is inverted; that which is properly pleasure, and ought to be pleasure to him, is become his torment, and no effort can render it otherwise.

Accordingly, in all our dealings with a sick man, and in all his thoughts respecting himself if he is capable of thinking truly, this inversion of his natural condition is recognised. It is remembered that what is properly pleasurable is painful to him, and that his pleasures are in things that should be to him worse than indifferent. When he is promised perfect enjoyment, he does not look forward to the perfecting of the kind of pleasure which he needs in his sickness, or of the ease which he then desires; not to perfect rest, to beds so soft that his limbs cannot ache upon them, or food that shall nourish with no demand upon the vital energy. He looks forward to a change in his own capacities whereby his enjoyment shall be made different.

In being promised ease, he is promised health; that is, to be able to find enjoyment, the true enjoyment of a man, in that which is pain to him, it may be intolerable and overwhelming pain; in exertion and endurance. He is to be delivered, by an increase or perfecting of his life, from pain, but by no means from all the things he feels as painful. The only possible condition of a true enjoyment is, that he shall find it in things that to him are painful; his only true deliverance is in an added power.

Now this thought, which sprang so naturally from our every-day experience, connected itself at once with the thoughts that have preceded. Is not man sick, falling short of his perfect life, and therefore feeling as pain that which is the rightful condition of his joy?

It is true, mankind are subject to pains, of body and of mind, which oftentimes are overwhelming, utterly beyond endurance, which

no effort, no philosophy, can render otherwise
than insupportable.   The woes which sur-
round human life often seem as if they could
not be exaggerated ; they seem to admit of
no consolation, no alleviation.   We cannot
rejoice in them ; we cannot rise above them.
They penetrate our very·hearts, and under-
mine the very sources of our strength.   But
though all this is true—though human misery
is immense—it does not follow that the whole
of it is not rightly the instrument and source
of happiness.   We see, in bodily disease, that
our feeling certain things utterly and intole-
rably painful, may arise not from evil in the
things themselves, but from want of a perfect
life in us ; they may be the very conditions of
natural and healthful pleasure.

And if we accept the thought of man as
sick, does not the whole fact of human wretchedness, the heavy total of the pains of men,
stand before us in this new light ?   Do we not
receive (a joyful gift) a perfect inversion of our
thought respecting it ?   All pains may be
summed up in sacrifice ; and sacrifice is—of
course it is—the instrument of joy.   To health,

to life, it is so. If it is not so to us, what does that mean, but that we are sick?

Man's life, his true and proper life, his health, is of such grandeur, of such intensity and scope, that it would absorb, and turn into the servitors of its joy, all that we now find intolerable pain, all agony and loss. Man's life is measured by his pains. It is such life, so large, so deep in consciousness, so rich in love, that in these sacrifices it can find its joy, its perfect satisfactions, its delights. These utter losses, and unfathomable miseries, and cruel strokes that leave us nothing, are its pleasurable efforts, its rejoicing gifts, its glad activities. So far short we fall; and so vast and glorious is the true human life. To apprehend it we must measure it by its pains, that is, by its capability of sacrifice. Man's being is cast on that scale, planned to that magnitude; it claims that intensity : a scope and an intensity that should make the uttermost evil and sacrifice to the self—intolerable evils to us now—but as the healthful exercise, the hearty toil, that make the limbs throb with exuberance of life.

So glorious is man's true being ; so high we should elevate our hopes. The life we shall receive is such as would make *all* sacrifices joy, even those extremest ones from which now we shrink most utterly. These things God hath prepared for them that love Him. It is true the height staggers our thought, and almost forbids our faith. Yet why should we shrink from it ? Are we not to be joined with Christ in His glory ; and is any height of joy in sacrifice, of power to give and to be glad in giving, too great for Him ?

And surely this thought of man's greatness is only like those new thoughts of greatness which the study of God's works everywhere enforces on us. Not less than immeasurably short of the reality fall all our natural thoughts of the Creator's works ; as in respect to nature, so also in respect to man. He, too, is unutterably greater than we believed, unutterably greater than we can conceive. But then God made him ; how, therefore, can any thought be too high or glad ? Man's perfect life could use all suffering for joy ; that is, a love for others should be so powerful within us, and a consciousness of other's good should be so fully ours, such rapture should possess us, that all loss, all griefs, should be to us the trivial sacrifices which love delights to have the opportunity to make. That they are not so now reveals the condition of the sick man, who needs, not ease or pleasure from without, but health within.

The evil of our pains should make us say, not how evil is this that we are called upon to bear, but how far short we fall—man falls—of the true human life, that this sacrifice is an evil to us. It should prompt us to seek deliverance, but deliverance by cure : the deliverance that is brought by a perfected life ; the joy that is the joy of love, and finds its necessary food in sacrifice. Any other thought of happiness, any other anticipation or desire, any antici-pation that puts aside the sacrifice, is as if a sick man should desire, not restoration, not the power of enjoying effort and absorbing endur-ance into pleasure, but only soft and easy couches, rest and shaded light. This is to fall short in our desires, to make disease our mea-sure, to demand a life that is not life, plea-

sures that are not truly pleasure. Must we
not aspire higher? Must we not seek, desire,
anticipate a happiness that is in giving; a life
that is so wide, and high, and full, that it can
take up, nay, must take up, all that is utterest
sacrifice to us, and make it the very condition
of its rejoicing energy?—a life to which it
would be as impossible to use our poor self-
pleasures, except for sacrifice, as it would be
to health to lead the life of sickness.

The whole thought is involved in the fact,
that devotedness and self-giving are the conditions of the joy of love; and that without
love the life that love leads joyfully were full
of pain. Man's perfect life is a life in which
love can be perfect, and find no limitation;
it is a life so truly lived in others, so partici-
pant with them, that utter and unbounded
sacrifice is possible; the limitations of this
mortal state bounding us no more. It is the
life of heaven. But the thought need not be
left vague. Do not the words of Scripture,
which speak of the union into oneness of those
who constitute the Church of Christ, supply to
it a definite basis? Are we not to share a life

wider and deeper than we now seem to possess ; a life co-extensive with Christ's body, in
the great joy of which all loss and sacrifice of
self is swallowed up ; the self remaining to us,
indeed, only as purified and ennobled into the
means of sacrifice ?*

Is not this, then, the standard of human
life ? Such life as would make all the bitter
pains, the unutterable losses and overpowering
agonies of man, the means of a glad service,
the rejoicing offerings of love ? We must
reckon, not the pains too great, but our life
marred. It is not dark, but the brightness of
a day that overwhelms our fevered eye. But
make us *whole*, and joy will banish pain.

* If this idea should seem obscure, it may be sufficient to
recall to our thoughts the representations given in Scripture
of the Divine Being, as dwelling, and acting, and living *in*
the creatures whom He regenerates.

CHAPTER VI.

WE can return now to the subject which forms the foundation of the thoughts that have been expressed ; namely, the redemption of man. If we recognise a want in our own nature, a condition like that of disease, making us feel pain in that which should be joyful, we feel at once that we have need of a deliverance, need of a cure. And seeing that this condition of want or disease affects not individuals only, but the whole human race, we feel that MAN needs a restoration, a perfecting of his life. Man's nature, appearing as diseased, claims a restorer ; appearing as the victim of a perverted feeling, which subjects it to evil, it needs to be redeemed from this.

Now this is the thought to which reference has been made in the idea of the redemption of the world. That redemption is the raising up of man from the evil condition in which he feels sacrifice as pain, into a condition in

which it is felt as joy, a condition of true
and perfect life.

Thus the idea stands in a definite light before us. This is the change which man's
nature needs : this is the change which it is
receiving. The redemption of man, as I have
spoken or shall speak of it here, means this
change ; a change not only of his feelings and
will, but of his actual state. I seek to regard
all our experience in its relation to this work ;
in the part which they bear in it I find the
glory of our pains and the consolation of our
griefs.

For if this work is being done, it is necessarily being done in all human experience ;
or rather, this experience of ours is that very
work itself. Strange and unlike it as they
may appear, these events which bring us joy
or sorrow, perplexity or pleasure, gain or loss;
these things in which we are actively engaged,
or which are passively inflicted on us ; these
are the carrying out of this work in man. So
that we may take up each one of our pains
and sorrows, and say, " Man's redemption is
carried out in this, is effected through it, de-

mands this to be." It is no matter that it is
so disconnected, so useless, so utterly insignificant. Nothing is disconnected; nothing that
moves man's spirit and rouses his capacity of
feeling is insignificant; nothing that is linked
—as all events are linked—inseparably into
the great history of man, is useless. If man's
redemption is a fact, it is the fact of these
experiences that may seem so small and ob-
jectless; the unseen fact of them, they seeming small only because it is unseen.

The evidence that this work is accomplished
is drawn, of course, from the declarations of
Scripture, which affirm a salvation bestowed
on man, and to be wrought out in him; which
promise that he shall be made alive in Christ,
and receive an eternal life. And here I may
briefly say that to my own mind the language
of the New Testament appears unequivocally
to affirm the redemption of all men; their
actual redemption from this evil and diseased
state in which we now are; the actual raising up of all to a perfect life. To my own
mind this universality seems to be clearly expressed in Scripture, and to give an unutter-

able delight to life. But it is not necessary
that this should be believed in order for us to
receive the happiness which the knowledge
that our sufferings serve their part in the great
work of redemption gives. That happiness
may still rest upon their serving the good of
others, though not all may share that good.
In the words before-quoted, St Paul says, "I
fill up that which is behind of the afflictions of
Christ for his body's sake, which is the church."
He does not say in this passage, as in so
many others he at least appears to say, that
the sphere of Christ's Church shall finally
include the whole human race. And the
happiness which flows from this thought may
be shared by those who can believe it true of
their own sufferings, even though they think
that those on whose behalf God uses them are
but a part and not the whole of men.

On this point I may venture one remark.
It seems to me that great difficulties have
been rightly felt in recognising in the language of Scripture any clear assertion that
all men shall be brought to Christ, and spirit-
ually made alive through Him. There is

much which, with thoughts such as ours have been, seems very expressly to affirm the contrary. But it appears to me that a chief source of these difficulties has been our own corruption. As we are now, we feel, and cannot help feeling, that of the two evils, pain and sin, pain, if it be extreme, is the greater. By nature we fear suffering more than sinning. Now, reading the New Testament with this feeling operating on our thoughts—as we are sure to do unless we are expressly on our guard against it—we can hardly fail to misunderstand its language, and to think of suffering or loss where it speaks of sin. So reading it, we may well see in its words mere hopeless ruin as the destiny of a large part of men. But if we keep watch over ourselves here, and remember that only he whose very life is death can feel suffering worse than sin, or could speak as if it were; if we remember that God's chief warnings, therefore, must be against, not what we fear most, but against that which, perhaps, we do not fear at all, the words of the New Testament present themselves to us in a new light. And the apparent meaning of many passages that we may easily recall, which speak as if Christ's kingdom were to embrace each member of the human race, telling us that He will draw all men to Him ; that every knee shall bow in His name ; that God shall be all in all ;—the apparent meaning of these passages may grow clear to our purged eyes as the true burden' of the gospel. ,We may be able, giving an awful force to all its threatenings, to take to our gladdened hearts—our hearts made warm with a new life—its large and joyful words, which speak of a salvation achieved for all, in all to be fulfilled ; a salvation of which one chief and most essential part consists in the very remedy of this perverted feeling. For when man finds only joy in sacrifice, there can no more be any evil felt by him as worse than sin. Sin, indeed, would stand as the one sole evil felt or capable of being felt by him, and in this would not his redemption be fulfilled ?

But while the belief that a redemption, a new creation of his nature, is being worked out in man, rests primarily and essentially on

the New Testament, yet it has other evidences
which may well add strength to our conviction.   True, it is a work that is unseen, a fact
that cannot be made visible to the eye of
sense, a fact which, save for its revelation in
Christ, could not have been discovered.   Yet
evidences of it may be found in many facts.
Surely in the very constitution of our nature,
made as it is for sacrifice, constructed to find
its chief joy only there, feeling, even in its
degradation, that no other joys are fully
worthy of it, proof is given that man is
designed and destined for a life proportioned
to his powers.

And do not the very pain and loss by
which man is surrounded, if we read them
rightly, testify to the same thing ?   Not acci-
dentally, not arbitrarily, do these assail him.
They are rooted in the essential conditions of
his being; they are inseparable from the structure of the world, and the relations which he
bears to it.   The individual must be sacrificed
and suffer loss.   It is his inevitable lot; the
total order of nature must be altered ere he
could escape it.   The necessity for sacrifice is

built into the structure of our being ; it is the birthright, the inalienable inheritance of life. What, then, can we say of it, but that it foretells and promises a state of being and a mode of life to which it shall not be alien and hostile ; a life in which it shall exist as a kindred and friendly element, and to the fulness of which it shall be minister, as we know it may be. Must not the inevitable existence of pain and loss, to us, mean this ?

And human history, when it is closely scanned, confirms the thought. Dark and unmeaning as it looks, this at least is visible in it, that without sacrifice no permanent satisfaction or truly good result is suffered to be attained. Incessantly man aims at ends which do not involve self-abandonment ; incessantly they are denied to him ; or, when gained, deceive his hope. Satisfaction is withheld ; the best founded hopes prove vain ; the highest powers fail ; experiments, on which the brightest expectations have been founded, fall in ruin ; no lesser end suffices ; but, by failure and discontent, man is driven ever onward. If we ask ourselves, To what goal ?

E

can we not well foresee the answer? He is
driven onward to this: to accept loving sacrifice as his good.

These facts are evident in human life even
as it is: that man is framed for joy in sacrifice; that until it can be made his joy, sacrifice
must be his torment, for it never can be banished; that without the willing acceptance of
sacrifice, no end is really answered in human
life, no satisfaction that is worthy of humanity
achieved. Add to these things the known
fact that our nature is imperfect, and the promise given of its renovation, and does not
their meaning become manifest?—that man's
redemption is the end for which this present
human life exists, the unseen end which it
achieves.

CHAPTER VII.*

IF we recognise that our *feeling* in respect
to sacrifice is inverted, and, as in sickness, the very condition of our rightful joy is
become the source of pain, we see that our
thought has also been perverted; we have
judged of good and evil falsely. And thus
does not light arise upon us, a light in which
we cannot but rejoice? Do not two mysteries
disappear: the mystery that God reveals
Himself in Christ, taking suffering and death
to show Himself to us; and the mystery of
the pain and sorrow of which our life is full?
Seeing what God's joy is, we see why Christ
alone can reveal Him. The nature of the joy
that is in love cannot otherwise be shown than
in taking sacrifice, and bearing sorrow. To
reveal God there must have been presented

---

* This chapter is partly a recapitulation.

to our eyes a Man of Sorrows, who chose and willingly embraced our griefs; for we feel that to be sorrow which is the very basis of His life and blessedness.

Nor could our human life be otherwise than full of sorrow too. We are dealt with—most happy those who most are dealt with so— according to the nature of our manhood, not according to our false feeling of it; according to the true good, not according to our perverted desires. *Our* good is secured in the felt loss; for our nature is larger than we feel: our ends are most subserved when most we feel them set at naught, for our destiny is higher than we know. The best is given us, though we would choose the worse: the basis of the largest and highest happiness, though we would choose the lower and the less. We are sacrificed, unwilling, for others' good, unseen: but it is no mystery that we are so; because in willing sacrifice for others' good, known, seen, and felt even as His own, lies God's own blessedness; the blessedness of all who truly can be blest. The broken remnants of the perfect life of joy are these: these pains, these multiplied and dire distresses, these clouds which to us veil the heavens in despair. Nor are they remnants only; they are germs from which the perfect life may grow; they are the omens of victory and delight; the basis upon which is to be built up a joy for which they cannot be too great. Of all that could not be spared from our life, our sacrifice is that which could be spared the least.

And that there is a perversion of man's feelings and desires, a radical want in our nature, is a known fact, proved long ago, and resting on evidence which needs no fresh confirmation. The disease of humanity has written its proofs on every page of history, has engraved itself indelibly on the human heart. The fact is already known, and we are justified therefore in using it to guide us. For his full life and happiness, man must be changed: we know it well. Surely, then, this change, to which we must look forward, may be one that shall make sacrifice his joy. Nay, for his perfect holiness and bliss, it must be so. For unless sacrifice is joy, holiness beyond temptation, and happiness without a sorrow, cannot be.

But if it thus proves itself to the reason that pain is sacrifice, and is good felt as evil through disease, it proves itself still more to the heart. Nothing can make pain so good as that it should be borne for others. So it becomes a privilege. And this is the inevitable demand of the human heart when it seeks for consolation. Even the natural feelings of men, unaided by that revelation of life which shows us this consecrated sorrow as its central fact, have often risen to confidence in the belief, and to happiness and strength based on it. The thought is beautifully expressed in the following passage by the Emperor Marcus Antoninus, showing that even in darkness and insufficiency, it is yet native to the soul :—

"Just as we must understand when it is said, that Æsculapius prescribed to this man horse-exercise, or bathing in cold water, or going without shoes ; so we must understand it when it is said, that the nature of the universe prescribed to this man disease or mutilation, or loss, or anything of the kind. For,

in the first place, 'prescribed' means something like this : he prescribed this for this man
as a thing adapted to procure health ; and, in
the second case, it means, that which happens
to (suits) every man is fixed in a manner for
him suitably to his destiny.   For this is what
we mean when we say that things are suitable
to us, as the workmen say of the squared
stones in walls or the pyramids, that they are
suitable when they fit one into another in some
kind of connexion.   For there is altogether
one fitness (or harmony.)   And as the universe is made up out of all bodies to be such
a body as it is, so out of all existing causes
necessity (destiny) is made up to be such as it
is.   And even those who are completely ignorant understand what I mean, for they say, It
(necessity, destiny) brought this to such a person.   This, then, was brought, and this was
prescribed to him.   Let us, then, receive these
things, as well as those which Æsculapius pre-
scribes.   Many, as a matter of course, even
among his prescriptions, are disagreeable, but
we accept them in hope of health.   Let the
perfecting and accomplishment of the things

which the common nature judges to be good,
be judged by thee to be of the same kind as
thy health. And so accept everything that happens, even if it seem disagreeable, because it
leads to this, to the health of the universe, and
to the prosperity and felicity of Zeus (the universe.) For he would not have brought on any
man what he has brought, if it were not use-
ful for the whole. Neither does the nature of
anything, whatever it may be, cause anything
which is not suitable to that which is directed
by it. For two reasons, then, it is right to be
contented with that which happens to thee ;
the one because it was done for thee, and prescribed for thee, and, in a manner, had reference to thee, originally from the most ancient
causes spun with thy destiny ; and the other,
because even that which comes severally to
any man is to the power which administers
the universe a cause of felicity and perfection,
nay, even of its continuance. For the integrity
of the whole is mutilated, if thou cuttest off
anything whatever from the conjunction, and
the continuity either of the parts or of the
causes. And thou dost cut off, as far as it is

in thy power, when thou art dissatisfied, and in a manner triest to put anything out of the way."*

And this feeling that the true consolation in distress must be found in its use and subservience to others' good, breaks out in a more exquisite and Christian form in Milton's poem on his blindness. Having heaped up the description of its distresses and privations, he turns, for his rejoicing in it, to this thought, and this only :—

" They also SERVE who only stand and wait."

And if they who stand and wait, do not those who suffer too ? Is it conceivable that God should give to some, whom He blesses with health and vigour and large gifts of influence, the privilege of greatly serving Him, of doing a wide work of use for others ; and that this privilege, which none else can equal or supply, He withholds from others from whom He takes health and strength, and every gift but that of suffering ? Does He give the one

* "The Thoughts of the Emperor Marcus Antoninus :" translated by George Long, p. 65.

the blessedness of *serving*, and refuse it to the
other?   " Behold, my ways are *equal*, saith
the Lord."

If our life were ordained to be good, truly,
satisfyingly good, it could be made so only in
one way.   It must be a life of sacrifice, for
all other goods fall short—we know they fall
infinitely short—of this ; and it must be sacrifice for unseen ends, because the best ends
must be unseen by us.   To be the best, our
life must be sacrifice, and for ends unseen.
It must be, therefore, to us, just what our life
is.   Must we not believe, then, that our life *is*
this : the best ?

In its fruitless-seeming pains and failures,
it fulfils the conditions of being the best life,
of presenting the highest form of good, and of
being turned to the best ends.   It is this God
calls upon us to believe ; this is a demand
He makes for faith, showing us, to justify and
confirm it, a life, like our own, of sorrow and
humiliation ; or if in this unlike our own, unlike only because the sorrow was greater, and
the humiliation more profound ; a life of sorrow in which the meaning and the end are no

more concealed, but made manifest to all. Revealing so the secret of our life, He calls on us for faith.

And so the pain of life is made good—all its pain ; not indeed to our sensuous feeling, but to that deeper feeling which rules and subordinates the other. This faith has power to make pain good ; to make us place above all price that which we most should shrink from. Only let the love be strong enough, and pain cannot be too great, nor loss too absolute.

And therefore, feeling that the heart here becomes the judge (the reason having given its assent,) appealing to the heart, to that moral feeling on which the existence of God Himself rests firm in man's belief, have we not answer, distinct and clear, that pain must be sacrifice ; a privilege, and not a loss ? Does not the thought, once seen to be possible, affirm itself as necessary, and refuse to be held in doubt ? Does it not link itself with the belief in God, so that we are compelled to say, that if God is, then pain is sacrifice —sacrifice for man ? For if we think other-

wise, then do we not choose to join evil with
His name ? Not to believe our pains serve
others' good, and are the fact of man's redemption, is but to disbelieve in God. It is
to doubt His goodness, and contradict the
very evidence on which we assert His being.
Once recognised in its true meaning, the
thought ceases to be a question of argument
and balanced evidence ; it sinks into the soul,
and becomes part of that deep conviction on
which all religion rests. Pain cannot be interpreted otherwise than thus, when once we see
that it can be thus interpreted. The heart
rises up from its chains and rejoices. God
has revealed Himself ; He has manifested joy,
and we see it and are glad. Amid our tears
we smile, for when our woes are deepest, then
our joys are highest. Then we are likest
Him, are nearest to the dignity of manhood ;
partakers most in that on which all living joy
is based, needing only that our life be perfected to make it joy.

We seek to be delivered from pain and
sorrow, and God designs to deliver us. Vainly
we seek, but He accomplishes. Our end is

not mistaken, but we mistake the means.
We seek deliverance by taking away; He
gives deliverance by adding;

> "'Tis life of which our nerves are scant,
> More life and fuller that we want;"

and God our Father, who knows our disease
and provides the remedy, leads us also to see
our need of it.

Surely it is not hard thus to turn and keep
our thoughts, recognising our own too narrow
life, and our too contracted heart therewith,
that makes us seek a good too small, and be
too easily content; that gives us a content
which cannot be undisturbed, desires which
God cannot gratify, because that would be to
curse instead of blessing; to curse instead of
blessing him for whom He has ordained the
highest blessedness. Surely it is not hard to
be on our guard against ourselves, and to
remember that our wanting and enfeebled
nature misleads us, makes us grasp at remedies that are no remedies, at goods that are
too small and pitiful for human good;—not
hard to aspire after more, and feel that our

only joy must be in that which we already know as the highest and the best. Surely we can learn to shape our prayer for health, not for alleviations ; for power to enjoy the good, not for the false goods our sickness can enjoy ; for power to rise up from man's false thought to God's true.

When, as reward, the prospect of our future grows into infinite glory, the thought of human nature rises into an elevation unconceived ; God appears before us infinite afresh in tenderness ; and the darkness of human sorrow, all the sad failure and agony of life, shining with the brightness of Christ's own sacrifice, are changed into the instruments and prophecies of joy.

Surely it is not hard to think ;—not, I want self-good to make me happy ; but, I want life to make sacrifice my joy ! And thus there is no mystery in pain. The world were an utter and hopeless mystery if pain were not. Where, then, would be the basis and the root of love, the prophecy of an enlarged and an ennobled nature ? where the revelation of our life in Christ ?

But there are some difficulties that will probably suggest themselves in respect to this thought. Two of these especially demand notice.

1. It may be felt that there can be no satisfactory treatment of the question of pain without a reference to sin. Is not sin the radical cause of all other evil, and without it would not man have had an entire immunity from suffering?

2. If we receive the thought that sacrifice is itself a good, and that painful things truly are the best, will it not lead us to voluntary choice and preference of pain to pleasure? In a word, would it not re-establish the long-disproved theory of asceticism?

In reference to the first of these questions very few words are required. So far from the connexion of pain with sin being called in question by the view that has been given, it is emphatically asserted. The whole thought consists in tracing out how pain arises and must arise from sin. From sin comes that diseased and wanting state of man whereby alone pain can be felt. Without sin pain had not been; for there had not been that perversion of feeling, and lack of life, whereby sacrifice is felt as pain. Pain is from sin, but sacrifice is not. The conditions of good and of happiness are not altered by it. These ever were to be found in sacrifice, and ever must be. Therefore it is that where sin has entered, and death by sin, pain must be.

And if it should be asked, How, then, did Christ become subject to pain, seeing that in Him was no sin? the answer is found in the fact that Christ took our infirmity; the disease of our nature was laid on Him, that He might remove it. He shared our feeling, that He might reveal the Father to us, and deliver us from the evil that He shared.

CHAPTER VIII.

BUT still this question remains: If the good of human life is found in that which we feel as painful, should we not seek pain rather than pleasure? Would not the acceptance of this idea lead us to the arbitrary choice of suffering, to the wilful giving up of all that makes life joyous, the abrogation of the sanctities of home, the deliberate extinction of all that civilises?

Though this question is naturally suggested by the thoughts which precede, nothing can be farther from their real spirit. It is because the things in which we find suffering are the sole condition of a full and perfect happiness that they are good. It is because life ought to be joyful that we have claimed this place, as joy-giver, for sorrow.

Pain is evil; it marks, and is token of, disease. It bespeaks want and loss. Thinking thus, we do not seek pain; we do not seek even to be resigned to it: we seek its utter

F

destruction, the doing away all possibility even
of its presence. Our hearts are avaricious,
rather, of delight, and refuse to be satisfied
with anything less than the utmost that we
can receive.

For, evidently, it is an entirely different
thing to say, Sacrifice is the good ; and to say,
Pain is good. The association of pain with
sacrifice, as we have seen—nay, as we know
so well by experiences, happily, we may believe, becoming more familiar in human life—
is unnecessary and partial, not constant and
inevitable. The true affinities of sacrifice are
with pleasure, with rapture even. It is only
by evil or want within, that sacrifice can be
otherwise than glad.

To dwell with joy, with deliberate choice, on
sacrifice, even to refuse to all else the rightful name of good, is not to praise or to sanc-
tion pain, but to affirm emphatically that it
ought not to be ; nay, that it ought not to be
possible. That to which it has attached itself,
the very root from which it seems to grow
(though not, in truth, does it grow from that
root, but from quite another, and it is a fatal

error which thus mistakes its source,) should yield the opposite. There should be no pain to man: from him, as he should be, sorrow and sighing should flee away—but not by the taking away of sacrifice.

If there be any difficulty felt here, the source of it will become quite manifest by recalling the illustration of sickness. Let us conceive, again, a sick man saying, "Alas! all motion of my limbs, all attempt to take exercise, is an intolerable pain to me; I cannot endure it;" and that the reply was made to him, "Courage, my dear friend; do not let yourself think of that as painful in itself, though it is exquisite and unendurable torture to you: that is the secret of the strong man's pleasure, and you shall come to have perfect and now almost inconceivable delight in it. Do not let yourself confuse the poor comfort, necessary as it may be to you, of sinking on your bed and lying still, with the true enjoyments of a man." Would this reply be thought a praise and recommendation of pain, or to advise the wilful choice of it? Surely not. It would simply be to encourage the sick man to keep his standard of pleasure high enough, and not to let it be degraded by his perverted feeling.

It is, in this respect, precisely the same thing when we rebuke ourselves for our false thoughts, and urge upon ourselves to recognise that, in the experience of suffering and loss which we feel even as unendurable distress, we must look for, and shall find, the source of joy.

In another way the true relations of this thought respecting pain may be illustrated. Let it be assumed that our object is joy, that this is the good at which we aim. Now here is in our life this fact of sacrifice, of individual suffering, opposing and preventing its perfect attainment; hurting, harming, often rendering joy impossible. Whence and what is the remedy to be? How is the hurtful thing to be rendered harmless, the mischief to be neutralised? Our whole knowledge of nature and of life concur in giving one answer: it must be turned to use. Things cease to hurt us then, and then only permanently, when they are made to serve our good. Nor can it be otherwise ; for nothing can be annihilated, nothing hindered from having, in some form or other, its full effect. The mere putting away or putting down evils has never succeeded. They return with a violence increased by the delay. The one condition upon which we can really avoid suffering by hurtful things is, that we should use them and make them serve us. A striking instance—though it is but an instance of a universal law—is given by the problem with which every large body of persons has to strive, of disposing of the waste materials of their life. Hurtful to a high degree, these waste materials are the source of inevitable disease if they are not put utterly away ? But how thus utterly put them away ? There is but one method that is truly efficient, and that is, to make them subservient to the increase of the means of life, to render them the fertilisers of our lands, the source of food. The drainage of towns will either poison or be an enormous tax, or it will feed. The condition of its ceasing to be an evil is, that it shall become a good. Necessarily it is so : its effects cannot be made null; our only choice is, shall they work our mischief or our benefit?

Now to point out that the noxious materials of our bodily life are in themselves a source of good, is not to encourage men to accept, or to deter them from removing, their ill effects. It is to open the path to their removal, and to stimulate the work. It substitutes for futile efforts at escape or suppression the rational plan of use.

It is such a change as this that would ensue in our practical life from the acceptance of the thought that sacrifice is the source of joy, and that it is associated with pain to us only by the want that is in ourselves. It would never prompt us to seek pain, never lead us to choose it for its own sake, never lead us to undervalue joy. It would make enjoyment more sacred in our eyes, would raise it to a holy significance, making it teach us lessons beyond itself. It is an image—feeble, partial, and too small though it be—of that which should be, in its perfection, universal in our life. It carries on our thoughts to a higher joy, that should be never absent, being fullest

in those portions of our life whence all joy
now is banished.

But further, this view not only guards us
from the arbitrary choice of pain, it enables
us to trace how that abuse arose, and whence
sprang that ascetic and self-denying spirit,
which, while not without its grandeur, has
inflicted so many injuries on men. Mankind
have always recognised a goodness in things
that are painful. In no time or place has the
feeling been wholly absent; but they have
not always understood the reason. It was not
recognised that these things are good only
because they are sacrifice, and subserve others'
welfare, and are therefore the true source of
gladness; that they are good in a familiar
and human sense, because they are adapted
to give joy. Hence men unavoidably mistook,
and attributed the goodness they could not
but recognise in them to that which is emphatically not good—to that which is the sign
of our own evil—the pain that was connected
with them. They ascribed to pain the goodness which belongs to sacrifice as the giver,
above all other things, of joy. A strange and

yet an inevitable inversion of thought, while the affections had not as yet fully recognised the joy that is in sacrifice, nor faith apprehended the relation of all human life to the unseen work that God does in man.

It was thus asceticism arose, seeking pain as good, self-denial as an end; and thus it failed. But the lesson it teaches remains for us. There is good in that which we find painful: the human soul does and will recognise it; nor can luxury, nor scorn, nor the history of innumerable ills wrought by pursuing pain, prevent. Man's soul recurs to it in spite of experience, in spite of enlightenment, in spite of ease.

Surely one thing alone can cure asceticism of its error, and free mankind from its dangers; and that is, to recognise the true nature of the good that is in sacrifice; that it is good, not for itself, nor because it involves pain, but precisely because it is not for itself, and is the true root of pleasure. If this be recognised, asceticism cannot again arise to distort life and tax humanity beyond its powers; the elements of our nature in which it has its root are turned into another channel, and find their satisfaction in deeds animated by another spirit.

A perfect guide, indeed, is given us thus in respect to the acts of sacrifice we should or should not undertake. Only that painful thing is good which has in it the root of pleasure. And this is that alone which serves others' good. Therefore no arbitrary, self-chosen sacrifice is good; there is no source of joy in that; it fails of the first condition. Only that sacrifice is good which either we accept for another's sake, ourselves seeing and choosing the result; or that which serves a like end unseen by us; and surely better serves a better end, being in God's hands, and not ours. For seen or unseen service sacrifice is good, but only when it is for service.

And this service either we accomplish for ourselves, or God works for us. We accomplish it when we consciously act from love or duty, and are blest in witnessing the service rendered. But God works it for us when He inflicts on us pains or losses; that is, when necessity enforces them, or right commands.

In these He is our minister, our Steward, to bestow better than we could do the service of our love. In sacrifices that we cannot escape, that come from Providence or deeds of men who in this are God's instruments, and in sacrifices for which He calls in duty, we recognise His hand, and know that they are used by Him. We feel our hearts glowing with a delight that humility does not forbid, "in this the Lord hath need of us." So far, He uses and blesses us, undertaking Himself to be the dispenser of our gifts.

The best in life, then, reading it by faith, as seeing the invisible (which not to do is blindness and self-chosen error,) the best in life is that part of it wherein there is inflicted on us, or rather accepted from us, inevitable sacrifice; it is in losses that we cannot escape, pains that God calls on us to bear, bafflings from which no effort can set us free, no uprightness deliver; or in that part of it wherein the voice of duty bids us incur loss or pain, or leave unacted the deeds that would delight us most. These things are the best in life; for these are God using us, these are His taking

our poor services—poor at the best, though
they may be great to us—and Himself using
them in ways too good, too deep and wide
for us to see. These are our contribution
to the redemption of the world, felt as painful because the sources of a joy too great,
which we make our own by freely yielding,
and accepting them ; thus making God's deed
ours. Must not this be the best in life,
the highest privilege? We link our weakness with omnipotence ; our blindness with
omniscience. This is the privilege of the
destitute, the sick, the feeble, of those who
are thwarted and cast down, who cannot save
themselves. Behold, to them too it is given
to save others.

Next to this privilege in goodness, among
the things that life can offer us, come the
sacrifices we can bear willingly for the good
of others ; less good, indeed, but seeming
more to us, a good that we can see, and
consciously subserve.

These are the portions of our life that rise
to the level of true goodness. Each yields
us joy in proportion to our love ; the greatest

privilege demanding for its joy, even because it is the greatest, faith as well as love.

Besides these, and separated from them by an immeasurable interval, there are the pleasures which are not of sacrifice, the pleasures of mere enjoyment: not truly good, yet not without their value. These are the portions of our life that cannot be employed for their best use; that our disability compels us to leave unturned to their true account; the alleviations which our sickness needs, and must bow itself to accept.

There are then, in this respect, three elements in our life :— First, the perfect good, which comes to us in the form of providential and inevitable sacrifice, or loss that right demands, on the full gladness of which we enter by faith, knowing in our hearts that which we cannot see. Next, there is the good, less, but still great and worthy of our manhood, the serving others consciously, and of our own free will, for ends within our sight, the joy of which is in proportion to our love. In this is included all honest and un-selfish work. And lastly, there are the pleasures we can gain for ourselves, the satisfactions of an individual kind with which our life is so abundantly surrounded. These last mark our feebleness and want ; but they are needful for us, and our enjoyment of them is essential. In so far as they give joy, they are types and reflections of the perfect life, though in a negative and inverse form. We understand their nature if we look on them as like the reliefs and perverted pleasures which the sick man demands ; not good, but to us necessary, and by us felt as good. This necessity and this feeling mark our disability, our need of a restored and perfect life.

And thus we see, from another point of view, the error of asceticism. The attempt to render man independent of self-enjoyment is an ignoring of his disease ; it is an attempt to act as if in health while health is wanting to us. It is not only our right, it is our duty to enjoy and to be happy. This is evident on all grounds. It is fitting to our state, and it is practically right. Pleasure does us good if gratefully and lovingly accepted ; the nature often expands and blossoms under it as under no other influence. And suffering oftentimes, not felt as the spring of joy it is, sours, cramps, and hardens. We cannot dispense with joy; we were never meant to dispense with it ; but we should seek it rightly.

Neither is there any tendency in the thought of sacrifice as the true source of joy to diminish the pleasurableness of that which we may call self-pleasure, or in any way to mar our natural enjoyments. It may, indeed, throw them into the shade, and relax somewhat (would to God it might !) the passion of our grasp upon them and pursuit after them ; but this is only by bringing them into the presence of another and superior pleasure. It is but as the boy less values childish sports as he grows into an appreciation of the serious gratifications of maturity, and sees that they have served their purpose in awakening capacities and calling forth desires they were never meant to fill.

CHAPTER IX.

TWO things might be here attempted: on the one hand, to trace farther the bearing of these thoughts upon our customary views; and on the other, to show how they might influence our life. But it seems better to leave them now untouched. These few pages have been written rather for some than for all, for those whom a special discipline may have prepared to welcome them; and to these I commit the thought, painfully conscious of my inability to say it as it should be said, an inability which those to whom I have written will at once feel most deeply, and most willingly forgive. To them I may say—for they whose tongues have often faltered and been dumb from very eagerness of passion, and dread lest any words, even the best, should spoil their story, will understand me—that great desire and fear have hindered me. These words I have stammered through; let them read, in their feebleness, reverence; a tribute to the sacredness of grief, made more sacred by the glory of its consolation.

I do not seek to show whether, or in what way, other thoughts, natural and perhaps established thoughts, might need to be modified in order not to conflict with these. There would probably be much less demand for change than might be supposed by those to whom the preceding thoughts may seem new. It may, however, serve to guard against mistake, if I say that of course no meritorious character is ascribed to human sufferings. Man's redemption is accomplished in them; not in any way by virtue of them; the restoration of humanity is carried out in our experience, not wrought by us. I need scarcely say that, because in these pages man's condition has been compared to that of disease, it is not to be supposed that other aspects of his state are not recognised, especially his sinfulness; or that Christ's work in relation to sin is lightly valued. But there has been the less reason for reference to these things, because I have left untouched the question of sin, and designedly limited myself to a

smaller problem. Hereafter light may perhaps be thrown even upon that profoundest
of all mysteries, man's revolt from God, and
deliberate choice of evil. I may perhaps be
pardoned for thinking that to understand
pain aright may tend to lessen, rather than
to aggravate, the difficulty of the greater
mystery of sin.

It may seem to some that more mention
should be made of pains that arise from sympathy, and so have their source in love. Let
me say that, as these are among the acutest
of human sufferings, an emphatic reference
has been made to them in that which has
preceded. Love can transform them, though
it gives them birth. While any loved ones
sorrow and are in distress, sympathy with
them must be sorrowful too ; but if *all* sacrifice is made joyful, then sympathy with
others' sacrifice will be sympathy with their
joy. These sorrows, also, man's perfect life
will turn into rejoicing.

In so far as these thoughts respecting pain
depend on a recognition of unseen ends served
by it, it seems to me that the recent ten-

dency of the human mind is wonderfully, and surely most happily, in harmony with them. What better could the students of Nature and the students of Humanity agree in telling us than this—their great lesson in these modern days—that the true essence and meaning of all things is hidden from our natural sight? What is this but to echo back the words we have so familiarly heard from childhood upward, till they have perhaps partly lost their force, which bid us live as seeing the invisible, and walk, not by sight but by faith? If this is the last lesson of science, it is also the first lesson of religion; perhaps now better to be learnt than ever before, and better understood, because reiterated from this new region, and enforced by this new evidence. To understand or feel our life aright, we must regard something not visible to ourselves: we must, in fact, be using faith. This, science tells us; this, philosophy. Shall they tell it to us in vain—to us who need so deeply to believe and act upon it, whose whole life is shrouded in darkness if it be not true, and may be, nay, must be, radiant with an unutterable glory and delight if it be true? Shall we refuse God's gifts because they come to us from unexpected quarters? shall we refuse to listen to this confirmation of the gladdest message, because it is given in unfamiliar tones?

And in respect to the practical bearing of these thoughts respecting pain, I refrain from speaking, partly because I feel incompetent, but more because I feel that it is not necessary. That they must have practical influence where they are truly felt, surely is evident: what influence they should have, perhaps, is better left to each person's heart than stated in another's words. If the thought can sink and take root in the soul, it will bear fruit; better fruit spontaneously than if conformed to any pattern. Nor, indeed, are circumstances so much alike in different cases that external actions can be conformed to special rules. This seems enough: a beautiful external life is the fruit of life within, especially of that life which dwells in joy. If joy could be brought to sorrow-stricken hearts, their path would blossom with good deeds; the gladness within

would overflow in acts of heroism and devotion, not uncalled for even yet.

And does not joy grow out of sorrow when
we see it thus—an infinite and tender joy
passing all other? Do we not feel the very
throbbings of God's heart, and see even this
sad world beautiful and good beyond concep-
tion, beyond hope; the poor, the miserable,
the blighted and shipwrecked lives clothed
with a sublimity grand, and yet exquisitely
tender, that pales before it the best joys of
earth, fair and blessed though they be? It is
good to be blest in health, and strength, and
family, and friends, and prospects, and suc-
cess; in capacity, and power, and scope for
usefulness; in love returned, and growing
with its return, giving and receiving more
with every year; in deeds of wide benefi-
cence which enrich the lives of nations. It
is good to be blest so; but not so good as
to be sacrificed, poor and wretched, halt and
maimed and bruised, heart-broken, spiritless,
incapable, lost utterly—so sacrificed for man's
redemption. That is to be like Christ; it is
to hear Him say, " Thou drinkest of my cup;

with my baptism art baptized. I make thee one with me, the destined sharer of my joy."

It is not too much; no, it is not too much; but it is more than can be given, save in utterest abasement. The head on which this bliss is poured must be bowed into the dust.

We cry in our agony, in weakness, failure, perplexity of heart, that there is no hope nor help. No hand seems to direct the storm, no pity listens. "God has forsaken us," we say. Do we say so, and not recall the words which fell in that great victory on Calvary—fell from the Conqueror's lips, "My God, my God, why hast thou forsaken me?" Blackness of darkness and despair, and sorrow blotting out God's hand, and feebleness sinking without a stay, these are not failure. In these characters was written first the charter of our deliverance; these are the characters in which it is renewed.

Ballantyne, Roberts, & Co., Printers, Edinburgh.

EXPOSITORY LECTURES ON ST PAUL'S EPISTLES TO THE CORINTHIANS.

Fourth Edition.   One thick volume.   Post 8vo, 10s. 6d.

"This volume will be a welcome gift to many an intelligent and devout mind. There are few of our modern questions, theological or ecclesiastical, that do not come up for discussion in the course of these Epistles to the Christians at Corinth."—*British Quarterly Review.*

LECTURES AND ADDRESSES ON LITERARY AND SOCIAL TOPICS.

New and cheaper Edition.   Fcp. 8vo, 5s.

"In each Lecture there is something to which we might take exception; but we feel that the man is giving us his belief, that his sympathies are in favour of whatever is lovely or of good report—that his is the faith, not of dogmatism, but of conviction, and we listen with warm admiration and esteem. The sterling value of the teaching, the liberality displayed in every line, more than compensate for any disadvantage the critic may discover."—*Daily News.*

ANALYSIS OF MR TENNYSON'S "IN MEMORIAM."

Fcp. 8vo, 2s.

——o——

MISS PARR (HOLME LEE.)

THE LIFE AND DEATH OF JEANNE D'ARC,
CALLED "THE MAID."

By Harriet Parr.   Two Vols.   Crown 8vo.

IN THE SILVER AGE.

Printed in Antique Type, on Tinted Paper.   With Two Illustrations.   Two Vols.   Crown 8vo, 12s.

. Cheaper Edition, One Vol., crown 8vo, with Frontispiece, 6s.

"Wise and beautiful essays. Readers not altogether under the influence of morbid craving for excitement will find wholesome recreation and the seeds of enduring happiness in their quaint humour, pensive quietude, subdued pathos, and courageous simplicity."—*Athenæum.*

"If such testimony were wanted, these volumes would be sufficient to stamp Holme Lee as a true lover of her kind, and the virtue could scarcely be illustrated in a more pleasant and profitable form. The book is full of bright painting, which gains in purity by the shadow that it casts."—*Reader.*

"The essays are carefully written, wise, tender, intelligent, full of charming descriptions of natural scenery, and, for the most part, frankly thought out."—*Illustrated Times.*

THE CROWN OF WILD OLIVE.

Three Lectures on Work, Traffic, and War.

By John Ruskin, M.A.   Fcp. 8vo.

THE ETHICS OF THE DUST.

Ten Lectures to Little Housewives on the Elements of
Crystallisation.   Crown 8vo, 5s.

"Mr Ruskin discourses of crystals, and from the ordering of crystals he
rises to the ordering of human life in its ethical relations.   It is needless to
say that every page of his writing is instinct with a fine feeling and fancy,
and lures us on to read by a rare delicacy of expression and freshness of
thought; but it may not be needless to add that this book, originally intended
for the young, will be not a whit less relished by the old."—*Times.*

"This is a book which does not degrade science to make it popular, or
insult the understanding by any red-riband morality.   It is pure, fresh, and
unhackneyed, in both treatment and subject-matter.   It has a higher fasci-
nation than a novel, because it does not cease when you lay it down, like the
music of a snapped cord, but suffuses itself over a large subject that invites
your loving, thoughtful, and patient study.   With girls, and boys too, we
hope it will supplant monogram and postage-stamp manias, and all the little
silly manias of little folks, by a crystal mania, with ethical readings, as we
are sure it will charm even older ones out of the mere 'eyeless manual labour'
of some darling but mechanical hobbies."—*Reader.*

SESAME AND LILIES.

Two Lectures delivered at Manchester in 1864.

I. OF KINGS' TREASURIES.   II. OF QUEENS' GARDENS.

Third Edition.

Fcap. 8vo, cloth, gilt edges, 3s. 6d.

"There is in these two Lectures a wealth of wisdom of the highest order,
conveyed in such words as none but John Ruskin knows how to use. . . . .
Seldom do we read anything so entirely good and so momentous in its teach-
ings as 'Sesame and Lilies.'   Such books have power, for they are full of
life.   We predict that Mr Ruskin's noble argument will not be ineffectual.
It is a golden gift-book for the daughters of England."—*Press.*

"Let as many as love earnestness and kindliness draw near and listen,
and whilst they smile, perhaps, at what they consider quaint, wild, unprac-
tical, acknowledge and lay to heart all—and it is much—that is good, and
true, and beautiful."—*Illustrated Times.*

—*o*—

J. BALDWIN BROWN, B.A.

THE HOME LIFE;

Or, Thoughts on the Christian Idea of Home.

By J. Baldwin Brown, B.A., Author of "The Soul's Exodus
and Pilgrimage," &c.   Crown 8vo.

LIFE IN NATURE.

By James Hinton.   Crown 8vo, 6s.

" It provides more welcome and profitable suggestions as to the real dignity of man, and the true destiny of nature, than we can afford to lose, and so eloquent and original a setting forth of it as we have here is certainly worthy of attention."—*Examiner.*

MAN AND HIS DWELLING-PLACE.

An Essay towards the Interpretation of Nature.

Second Edition.   Crown 8vo, 6s.

" Much the most powerful, and by far the most complete work of the kind we have seen."—*Saturday Review.*

"A most original, acute, well-expressed, and altogether remarkable book, distinguished not more by originality than by piety, earnestness, and eloquence."—*Fraser's Magazine.*

—o—

ARISTOTLE.

A Chapter from the History of Science, including Analyses of Aristotle's Scientific Writings.

By George Henry Lewes.   Demy 8vo, 15s.

"We recommend the work to the consideration of those who are able to appreciate the vast amount of scholastic research displayed, and the sound philosophical principles enunciated by Mr Lewes, to whom for this fresh effort the literary world owes another debt of gratitude."—*Press.*

THE LIFE OF GOETHE.

A New Edition.   Partly Re-written.   With a Portrait.

One Volume.   Demy 8vo, 16s.

"One of the best biographies in English, or in any other language."— *Saturday Review.*

" Mr Lewes's biography of Goethe may be said to have now definitively taken its place among the classics of our generation."—*Reader.*

" Few writers have been more happy in the choice of a hero, and few men of genius have been more fortunate in a biographer."—*Press.*

STUDIES IN ANIMAL LIFE.

With Coloured Frontispiece, and other Illustrations.

Crown 8vo, 5s.

" This book will be a good companion to those who are lounging by the sea-side, giving them an interest in polypes and molluscs.   Those again who are spending their summer near breezy English commons will find Mr Lewes a pleasant guide in their rambles."—*John Bull.*

MR SAVORY.

ON LIFE AND DEATH.

Four Lectures, delivered at the Royal Institution of Great Britain.

By William S. Savory, F.R.S., Assistant-Surgeon to, and Lecturer on Anatomy and Physiology at, St Bartholomew's Hospital. Crown 8vo, 5s.

" A well-written and most interesting little treatise on matters, a knowledge of which must be of importance to every one."—*Westminster Review.*

—o—

REV. S. BARING-GOULD, M.A.

THE BOOK OF WERE-WOLVES:

Being an Account of a Terrible Superstition.

By Sabine Baring-Gould, M.A., Author of "Iceland : Its Scenes and Sagas." With Frontispiece. Crown 8vo, 7s. 6d.

" Mr Baring-Gould has presented us with a curious and highly interesting monograph upon *Were-Wolves*, and the folk-lore connected with lycanthropy, or the various forms under which the notion of a wolf-fiend or man-wolf has existed in different countries. Mr Baring-Gould's extensive knowledge of Icelandic literature has enabled him to fortify his argument at every point with illustrations which make his little volume one of genuine entertainment."—*Saturday Review.*

" In this remarkable little book, remarkable for a power its external aspect does not promise, and an interest its name will not create, Mr Baring-Gould, an author known hitherto chiefly by his researches in Northern literature, investigates a belief once general in Europe, and even now entertained by the majority of the uneducated classes."—*Spectator.*

" This is a very curious book on a very curious subject. To the elucidation of the theme Mr Gould has brought to bear much erudition and research. . . . . To the student of popular superstitions and folk-lore the earlier chapters of the present work will be most interesting, much valuable information as to the origin of words and the affinity of languages being incidentally given."—*Illustrated Times.*

ICELAND: ITS SCENES AND SAGAS.

With 35 Illustrations and a Map. Royal 8vo, gilt edges, 10s. 6d.

" An extremely handsome and attractive volume."—*Guardian.*

" This magnificent book is well worthy of all the praise which has been lavished upon it by the public. . . . . We believe the book will become a standard work of our libraries; and its exterior is as well fitted for the boudoir as its interior is for the study of the student."—*John Bull.*

BARON VON WOLZOGEN.

RAPHAEL: HIS LIFE AND HIS WORKS.

By Alfred Baron von Wolzogen.   Translated by F. E. Bunnètt.

With Photographic Portrait.   Crown 8vo, 9s.

" This volume purports to be a concise summary of the most important investigations and decisions hitherto arrived at with regard to the great master of painting. The author's view of the multifarious Raphael literature seems to be, that even the most complete works have laid too little stress upon their hero's mission as regards the history of civilisation, and upon the importance of his art, both philosophically and historically.   The present work contains a complete history of the life of Raphael, comprised in as short a compass as the subject will admit of. There is much to praise in the research and ability displayed in detailing the many paintings which by this time have become scattered over Europe. We shall here find a reference to all the well-known paintings, with their historical origin, their subsequent adventures, and their present position.   There are plenty of interesting historical events scattered through the volume, which will rank as an excellent history of Raphael's life and a compendium of his works."—*Observer.*

——o——

HERMAN GRIMM.

LIFE OF MICHAEL ANGELO.

By Herman Grimm.   Translated by F. E. Bunnètt, Translator of Gervinus's " Shakespeare Commentaries."

With a Photographic Portrait from the Picture in the Vatican.
2 vols. crown 8vo, 24s.

" Herman Grimm has executed his task as a labour of love, ransacking all the museums of Europe for evidence on the life of his hero, but using his vast material rather to enrich and lighten his own narrative, than to solidify it in the true German style. His biography, admirably translated by Miss Bunnètt, is as full of point and sparkle as a French memoir, as crowded with anecdote as an English book of reminiscences, but pervaded throughout with that historic instinct, that power of seeing as well as describing the picture called up by a host of minute facts, which is the first merit of the German biographer. . . . . Herman Grimm has displayed a German's laboriousness in collecting materials, which he has used with a Frenchman's lucidity and ease; his work is full of most thoughtful and true criticism of art, and his narrative has been rendered into English as easy, and yet as characteristic, as if he himself had been accustomed to think in our tongue."—*Spectator.*

LONDON : SMITH, ELDER & CO., 65 CORNHILL.